Kiviuq and the Bee Woman

By Noel McDermott   Illustrated by Toma Feizo Gas

INHABIT
MEDIA

"*Sininnaqsijuq*," I say to my grandchildren. "It is time for sleeping, little children."

At this time of night, they always ask, "*Ataatatsiaq, unikkaaqtuarutilauqtigut!* Grandfather, please tell us a story!"

"If you listen attentively, I will," I say. "What story would you like? Would you like to hear about Takannaaluk, who controls all the animals and lives deep under the sea?"

"No, we don't want to hear about Takannaaluk!" they say. "We want to know what happened to Kiviuq!"

"What about the story of the orphan boy who became strong and defeated all his enemies?"

"No! We want to hear about Kiviuq!"

Very well. If that's what they want, I will tell another of Kiviuq's adventures. "Have I told you about Kiviuq's meeting with Iguttarjuaq, the Bee Woman?"

"No, we have never heard about Iguttarjuaq. Please tell us that one!" they beg.

"*Naammaktuq*, very well. *Naalaktiaritsi*, listen carefully...." And so I begin.

When we were last with Kiviuq, he had just escaped from the *tuutaliit*, the deadly mermaids. After getting to dry land and making sure there were no mermaids about, he set up his little *tupiq*, his sealskin tent, and tried to sleep. But he had difficulty sleeping because in his dreams, he saw the fierce and angry faces of the tuutaliit as they tried to tear his *qajaq* to shreds with their long, sharp nails.

When he eventually awoke, Kiviuq sat by the shore and scanned the sea for any signs of the deadly tuutaliit. He shivered to think of them. But all he could see was the calm ocean, the blue sky, and some *naujaat*, sea birds, looking for scraps to eat.

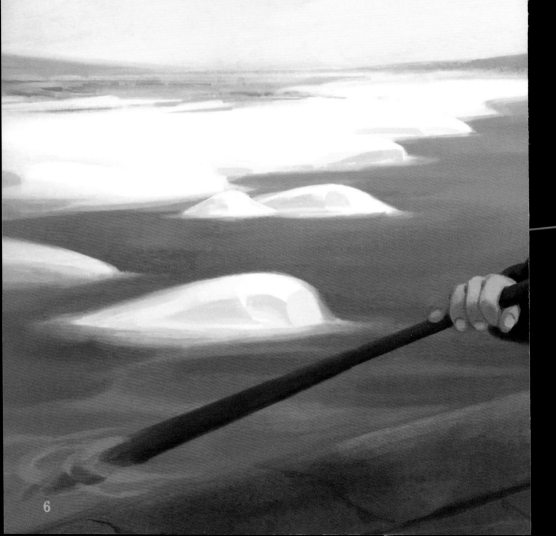

Kiviuq knew that if he wished to find his way home, he would have to travel by sea. There was no other way. He could not stay in this place indefinitely. Winter would soon be here, and already there was a very thin layer of ice forming on the sea.

As the day was so fine and he was reluctant to take a chance on the deep water, Kiviuq decided to paddle close to the shore.

This way he could keep an eye out for any tuutaliit that might come his way. Perhaps he would even meet some Inuit who might be able to tell him in which direction his own camp lay.

And so, Kiviuq packed some meat into a bag and, feeling much better than he had before, with the warmth of the *siqiniq*, the sun, on his back, he set off in his qajaq along the shore.

Kiviuq journeyed for a long, long time without seeing any Inuit or animals. It was as if the whole world had gone into hiding. He was feeling hot and tired and hungry, so he decided to stop and make camp for the night.

Suddenly, he spotted something in the distance that looked like a tupiq. As he paddled toward it, Kiviuq strained to see what the structure was. When he got close enough to see, the tiredness drained from his body, and

he felt like singing. It was a *tupiq*! Kiviuq was
overjoyed. After all that had happened to him,
now he could relax and share his adventures
and his *niqi*, his food, with another human
being.

Kiviuq stepped out of his qajaq and pulled it up onto the shore. All his tiredness now gone, Kiviuq eagerly approached the tupiq, but as he got closer, something told him to be cautious and not to startle the Inuit who lived in the tent. The inhabitants might be sleeping and might not like being disturbed by a stranger.

Sometimes strangers can be dangerous, especially if they are *tuurngait*, spirit helpers, doing mischief on behalf of a malicious *angakkuq*, a shaman.

When Kiviuq got right up to the tupiq, he listened for a while but could hear nothing, just the sound of the *anuri*, the wind, coming off the sea. Lifting a flap on the side of the tupiq, Kiviuq quietly looked inside.

Inside the tupiq, Kiviuq saw a very large woman who seemed to be skinning a *natsiq*, a seal. Something about her made Kiviuq nervous. Not wanting to confront her, he started spitting at her to get her attention.

At first, the woman ignored Kiviuq, but after a while, without looking up, she said, "What normally doesn't drip is dripping." Her words startled Kiviuq. Then, slowly, the woman lifted up her head and looked at Kiviuq. To his surprise, Kiviuq noticed that the folds of the woman's eyelids completely covered her eyes. She couldn't see Kiviuq. She couldn't see anything at all.

The woman spoke very nicely to Kiviuq and said, "Why don't you come into my tent? You must be very tired after your long journey. Look at the state of your clothes. They are all torn and wet. Let me dry and mend them for you, Kiviuq."

"*Qujannamiik*, thank you," he said, although he felt it strange that this woman knew his name.

Taking Kiviuq by his arm, she helped him onto the sleeping platform at the back of the tent. "There," she said, "you can rest easily now. I will put your clothes on the drying rack, and they will be dry in no time. While you sleep, I will go and get some more firewood."

The woman went out, and Kiviuq settled down comfortably to sleep. He didn't know that the large woman was Iguttarjuaq, the Bee Woman, an ancient bee in human form who captures unsuspecting travellers, skins them, cuts them up, puts them in a pot, and boils them. She intended to kill Kiviuq, cook him, and eat him!

Kiviuq tried to sleep, but something about the large woman made him uneasy. He decided to get away from there. But just as he was about to run away, the woman returned. Sitting down, she took her very large *ulu*, her knife, and sliced off both her eyelids. She stared at Kiviuq. Her eyes, large and moon-shaped like those of an insect, scared him half to death. Kiviuq was rooted to the spot. Then, without saying a word, the large woman popped the eyelids into her mouth and began to chew on them.

In the centre of the tupiq was a big cooking pot. To his horror, Kiviuq realized the woman was boiling human meat. The seal Kiviuq thought she was skinning was actually a human. Kiviuq was horrified and shouted, "*Inungujuq!* It's a human! *Inungujuq!*" Frightened out of his wits, Kiviuq fainted and fell back onto the sleeping platform.

When he awoke, Kiviuq looked around, but the large woman was nowhere to be seen. Looking around the tupiq, Kiviuq was shocked to see human skulls lined up along the back of the sleeping platform.

One skull said to him, "You are going to end up like me if you don't get away. Put on your clothes and go right now." The other skulls all spoke at once, chattering in agreement.

Kiviuq didn't hesitate. Quickly, he grabbed his *atigi*, his jacket, and his *qarliik*, his pants, and put them on. Then he reached for his *kamiik*, his boots, but the drying rack kept moving out of his reach. He tried desperately to get to his kamiik, but the rack just moved away each time. Kiviuq was desperate to get away before the Bee Woman came back.

Now, I have told you before how all Inuit have a *tuurngaq* or helping spirit they can call to come to their aid in times of trouble, and this was one of those times. Kiviuq really needed help. Suddenly, into the tent flew an *amauligaq*, a snow bunting, which headed right for the drying rack and knocked it over so that Kiviuq's kamiik fell onto the floor of the tent.

In a flash, Kiviuq grabbed his kamiik and ran to the door. But there was the Bee Woman, barring his way. She slashed at Kiviuq with her sharp ulu, and he feinted quickly to his left, just barely avoiding being cut to pieces. Kiviuq could see no way out.

Suddenly, Kiviuq heard a great roar in the distance. He recognized the sound immediately. It was the spirit of *nanuq* the polar bear. The roar grew louder and louder until it was right outside the tent. The Bee Woman disappeared as if by magic.

Kiviuq tried to open the door. It was shut tight, as if someone or something was forcing it closed. He pulled and pulled, and finally the door opened. As he ran through the opening, the door slammed shut, tearing off the tail of his atigi. He ran as fast as a caribou toward the beach, where he had left his qajaq. He could hear footsteps behind him, but he didn't dare look back. He got to the qajaq, picked it up, and ran to the water, taking a quick look behind him to see where the Bee Woman was.

The Bee Woman had paused to put on her qarliik. Then, to show her anger and her power, and to frighten Kiviuq, she took her ulu and split a rock into two pieces. She shouted, "I am Iguttarjuaq, the Bee Woman, and I am going to kill you with my ulu."

Kiviuq was paddling furiously away from the shore when, with a sharp and sudden jolt, he was stopped in his tracks. The Bee Woman had caused the sea to freeze all around Kiviuq's qajaq. He was stuck in ice with no way to escape out to the open water. "What are you going to do now?" the Bee Woman called out to Kiviuq. "There is no way out."

Some Inuit say that Kiviuq was an angakkuq and had power of his own, and maybe he had. He took his harpoon and struck the ice a mighty blow so that it split apart, allowing him to paddle his qajaq in the open water along the shore. But he was not out of danger yet.

"If you were in the water, I would have harpooned you," Kiviuq yelled at the Bee Woman in defiance. She just said, *"Uhuuu, uhuuu,"* and continued walking along the shore, following Kiviuq as he paddled away.

Kiviuq was paddling with all his might, desperately trying to get away from the terrible Bee Woman. He knew that if she caught him, he would end up in the cooking pot like all the others.

Kiviuq was heading for a point of land he could see in the distance. He felt if he got there before the Bee Woman, he would be safe. But once again, she took her ulu and smote the air in front of her, and all at once the sea began to freeze around Kiviuq. He was in real trouble now.

He was dead tired from all his exertions. He could hardly summon another drop of energy from his body, and the more he paddled, the more he got stuck in the fast-freezing ice.

The land seemed to be floating before him, but
there was no way he could reach the point of land
before the Bee Woman, who was moving along
the shore with remarkable speed. Suddenly Kiviuq
remembered an *irinaliuti*, a magic song he had learned
years ago, which had helped him when he had been in
danger before. With a loud voice, he began to sing, and
as he sang, all at once the ice began to part, allowing
Kiviuq to reach open water and safety.

   He looked toward the land and could just make
out the figure of the Bee Woman standing and
looking out to sea. He stopped paddling and rested
until the sky began to darken. Then he quietly made

his way toward the shore, keeping a lookout for tuutaliit in the water and the Bee Woman on the land. He felt this would be another restless night.

As for Iguttarjuaq, the Bee Woman, she slowly went back home to await the next unsuspecting visitor.

That's all I can remember, for now: *taima*.

Glossary of Inuktitut terms

amauligaq
(pronounced "ama-o-li-gaq") — snow bunting

angakkuq
(pronounced "an-ga-kook") — shaman

anuri
(pronounced "a-no-ri") — wind

ataatatsiaq
(pronounced "a-taa-tat-see-ak") — grandfather

atigi
(pronounced "a-te-ge") — jacket

inungujuq
(pronounced "i-noo-ngo-juq") — word meaning "it's a human"

irinaliuti
(pronounced "er-e-na-lee-oo-te") — a magic song or chant

kamiik
(pronounced "ka-miik") — a pair of boots

naalaktiaritsi
(pronounced "naa-lak te-a-ret-se") — word meaning "listen carefully"

naammaktuq
(pronounced "naam-mak-toq") — word meaning "very well"

nanuq
(pronounced "na-nook") — polar bear

natsiq
(pronounced "nat-sek") — seal

naujaat
(pronounced "na-o-jaat") — sea birds

niqi
(pronounced "ne-qe") — food

qajaq
(pronounced "ka-yak") — kayak, a one-man boat

qarliik
(pronounced "qar-leek") — pants

qujannamiik
(pronounced "qo-jan-na-meek") — word meaning "thank you"

sininnaqsijuq
(pronounced "se-nen-naq-se-joq") — word meaning "it is time for sleeping"

siqiniq
(pronounced "si-qi-niq") — sun

taima
(pronounced "ta-ee-ma") — the end

tupiq
(pronounced "to-piq") — tent

tuurngait
(pronounced "toor-nga-it") — many spirit helpers

tuurngaq
(pronounced "tuur-nga-q") — a spirit helper

tuutaliit
(pronounced "too-ta-leet") — many mermaids

ulu
(pronounced "u-lu") — woman's knife

unikkaaqtuarutilauqtigut
(pronounced "o-nik-kaaq-to-a-ro-te-lauq-te-gut") — word meaning "tell us a story"

Contributors

Noel McDermott

Noel McDermott is a retired professor of literature at
Nunavut Arctic College in Iqaluit, Nunavut, where he
lived and taught in Inuktitut and English for thirty-five
years as a classroom teacher, school principal, and lecturer
in the teacher training program. He has held teaching
appointments at many other educational institutions,
including McGill University, Trent University, and the
University of Waterloo, as well as at the Sami University
in Kautokeino, Norway. He presently teaches introductory
Inuktitut courses at Queen's University in Kingston, Ontario.
His previous books are *Akinirmut Unipkaaqtuat: Stories of
Revenge* and *Kivuq and the Mermaids*.

Toma Feizo Gas

From his earliest days of reading sci-fi and fantasy books,
Toma has been fascinated with the dramatic scenes
portrayed on the covers of those books. There started his
lifelong love affair with telling stories through pictures.
Today, Toma's key influence remains the people in these
stories, the motives that drive us, and the decisions that
shape us, propelling him to craft bold visual statements
and contrast in his own art. As a career illustrator, his work
can be found gracing the pages and covers of titles for the
Dungeons & Dragons, Pathfinder, Star Wars, and *Mutant
Chronicles* role-playing games, as well as several fantasy
novel series.

Published by Inhabit Media Inc. · www.inhabitmedia.com

Inhabit Media Inc. (Iqaluit) P.O. Box 11125, Iqaluit, Nunavut, X0A 1H0
(Toronto) 191 Eglinton Avenue East, Suite 310, Toronto, Ontario, M4P 1K1

Design and layout copyright © 2019 Inhabit Media Inc.
Text copyright © 2019 Noel McDermott
Illustrations by Toma Feizo Gas copyright © 2019 Inhabit Media Inc.

Editors: Neil Christopher, Kelly Ward, and Grace Shaw
Art director: Danny Christopher
Designers: Astrid Arijanto and Sam Tse

We acknowledge the support of the Canada Council for the Arts for our publishing
program.

This project was made possible in part by the Government of Canada.

ISBN: 978-1-77227-215-4
Printed in Canada

Library and Archives Canada Cataloguing in Publication

McDermott, Noel, author
      Kiviuq and the bee woman / by Noel McDermott ; illustrated by Toma Feizo Gas

ISBN 978-1-77227-215-4 (hardcover)

      1. Kiviuq (Legendary character)--Juvenile fiction. 2. Bees--Juvenile
fiction. I. Gas, Toma Feizo, illustrator II. Title.

PS8625.D44K48 2018   jC813'.6   C2018-905481-6